The Little Girls' Picnic Surprise

Illustrated by J.-L. Macias S.
Retold by J. Carruth

Karen and Katy often visit with each other. They are best friends. Today they are giving their dolls a bubble bath. Michael would like to help but he is not wanted. So he hides behind a bush.

Bathing the dolls and washing their clothes takes a long time. But when they are finished, Karen and Katy sit down to a lovely picnic. "I wish they would let me join them," Michael thinks, as he watches. "I do feel hungry." Then he has a super idea.

He runs back home for the wolf mask he keeps in his toybox. When **Karen** and **Katy** see the fierce wolf grinning at them, they run away.

Naughty boy! Michael then helps himself to a large piece of cake. No wonder the girls are furious with him. "First you scare us," Karen says, "and now you are eating our food!"

Michael eats so much that he feels sleepy. "Let's scare him," says Katy. And they dress their dolls in weird, scary looking hats. When Michael wakes up he thinks he is in the middle of a terrible nightmare. "Leave me alone!" he cries.

The two friends see that he is frightened and tell him, "It is only our dolls in funny hats." Michael says he is sorry for spoiling their picnic. "I won't bother you again," he says. "I'm going home."

At the end of their busy day, Karen and Katy get ready for bed. "We can let Michael play with us tomorrow," Karen says. "Tomorrow can be fun!"

First Karen yawns and climbs into her bunk. Then Katy yawns. Sleep well, both of you!

Published in the United States and simultaneously in Canada by Joshua Morris.
431 Post Road East, Westport, CT 06
Printed in Belg